The Bremen-town Music

Retold from Grimm
by RUTH BELOV GROSS

Pictures by JACK KENT

SCHOLASTIC INC.
New York Toronto London Auckland Sydney

ISBN 0-590-33835-8

Text copyright © 1974 by Ruth Belov Gross.
Illustrations copyright © 1974 by Jack Kent.
All rights reserved. Published by Scholastic Inc.

12 11 10 9 8 7 6 5 4   8 9/8 0/9

Printed in the U.S.A.   24

For Joel Belov, my first musician

There was once a donkey
who was getting old.
One day he heard his master say,
"That donkey is too old to work.
So why should I feed him?"

"If he won't feed me," thought the donkey,
"I will run away.
Maybe I can't work for him any more.
But I'm good at music.
I will go to Bremen-town
and be a musician there."

And the donkey set out
for Bremen-town.

BREMEN

ROTENBURG

VERDEN

5

On the way he met a dog.

"What's wrong?" said the donkey.
"You are out of breath."

"I am getting too old to hunt,"
said the dog. "I heard my master
say he wanted to kill me.
So I ran away.
But what shall I do now?"

6

"I know what," said the donkey.
"I am going to Bremen-town
 to make a little music.
 I can bray, and you can bark.
 Come with me to Bremen-town.
 We'll be musicians there."

So off they went to Bremen-town.

Soon they met a cat.

"What's wrong?" said the donkey.
"You look as sad as a rainy day."

"Why should I look happy?" said the cat.
"I am getting too old to run after mice.
I heard my mistress say
she was going to drown me.
So I ran away.
But what shall I do now?"

"You are good at night-singing,"
said the donkey.
"Come with us to Bremen-town.
We'll be musicians there."

So off they went to Bremen-town.

Soon they met a rooster.
"What's wrong with you?" said the donkey.
"The way you crow! It makes me want to cry."

"I am crowing while I can,"
said the rooster. "I heard my mistress say
she was going to cut off my head
and put me in the soup."

"You have a fine voice,"
 said the donkey.
"Come with us to Bremen-town.
 We'll be musicians there."

So off they went,
 the donkey
 the dog
 the cat
 and the rooster.

At night they came to a forest.
It was dark, and they were ready
to go to sleep.

The rooster looked around.
"I see a light," he said.
"There must be a house
near here."

"A house!"
said the donkey.
"Let's go!"

So off they went.

Before long they came to the house.
The donkey looked in the window.

"What do you see?" said the rooster.

"What do I see?" said the donkey.
"I see a table full of good things to eat.
 And I see robbers at the table.
 They are eating and having a good time."

"I'd like some of that food," said the rooster.
"So would I," said the dog.
"But how can we get rid of the robbers?"

"Let's all think," said the donkey.
They all thought hard.

And soon they were ready.

"All together now," said the donkey.
"One, two, three...."

HEE-HAW
BOW-WOW
ME-OW
COCK-A-DOODLE-DOO

And they came
crashing through
the window.

The robbers ran away.

And the four friends ate and ate.

Then they put out the lights
and went to sleep.

The robbers were hiding
in the forest all this time.
"Why did we run away?" they said.
"There's nothing to be afraid of."

But they sent one robber back
to make sure.

The robber went into the house.
He saw the cat's eyes shining in the dark.
"Ah!" said the robber. "I see that
there are still some coals burning
in the fireplace. I will use them
to light my candle."

The robber went right up to the cat.
The cat spit at him and scratched his face.

"Help! Help!" said the robber.
And he ran to the door.

The dog jumped up
and bit the robber's leg.

"Help! Help!" said the robber.
And he ran outside.

The donkey woke up and gave the robber
a good hard kick.

"Help! Help!" said the robber.

The noise woke the rooster up.
Cock-a-doodle-doo!
COCK-A-DOODLE-DOO!

The robber ran away from the house
as fast as he could.
"Help! Help!" he cried.

"What happened?" the other robbers
 asked him.

"Oh," he said, "a horrible witch
 spit at me.
 She scratched my face
 with her sharp nails.
 Then a monster near the door
 stabbed my leg with a knife.
 And then a giant hit me with a club.
 And a ghost screamed at me."

The robbers never went back to that house again.

But the donkey
and the cat
and the dog
and the rooster
liked the house so much
that they stayed forever.

They never went to Bremen-town
to be musicians there.